Smoked Gouda Murder

Book Five

in

Papa Pacelli's

Pizzeria Series

By

Patti Benning

Author's Note: On the next page, you'll find out how to access all of my books easily, as well as locate books by best-selling author, Summer Prescott. I'd love to hear your thoughts on my books, the storylines, and anything else that you'd like to comment on – reader feedback is very important to me. Please see the following page for my publisher's contact information. If you'd like to be on her list of "folks to contact" with updates, release and sales notifications, etc...just shoot her an email and let her know. Thanks for reading!

Also...

...if you're looking for more great reads, from me and Summer, check out the Summer Prescott Publishing Book Catalog:

http://summerprescottbooks.com/book-catalog/ for some truly delicious stories.

Contact Info for Summer Prescott Publishing:

Twitter: @summerprescott1

Blog and Book Catalog: http://summerprescottbooks.com

Email: summer.prescott.cozies@gmail.com

And...look up The Summer Prescott Fan Page on Facebook – let's be friends!

If you're an author and are interested in publishing with Summer Prescott Books – please send Summer an email and she'll send you submission guidelines.

TABLE OF CONTENTS

SMOKED GOUDA
MURDER

Book Five in Papa Pacelli's Pizzeria Series

CHAPTER ONE

Eleanora Pacelli pushed through the employee entrance into Papa Pacelli's Pizzeria with a box in her arms so big that she couldn't see anything in front of her. Judging by the exclamation that followed soon after, she had almost run into one of her employees.

"Sorry," she called out.

"Here, let me help."

Someone grabbed the box from the other side and helped her maneuver it through the door. Ellie recognized Clara's bushy hair. Together, they carried the box across the kitchen and put it on the table in the corner that she and her employees ate lunch at.

"Thanks," she said.

"No problem." Clara brushed her hands off and put them on her hips, giving the box a quizzical look. "What's inside?"

"Thanksgiving decorations," Ellie told her. "I thought the pizzeria could use some dressing up. It's looked so bland since we took the Halloween decorations down."

"That's a lot of decorations."

"Well some of them are seasonal and should be able to stay up until we start decorating for Christmas. Come on, give me a hand and we'll start putting them up."

Ellie had spent the weekend picking up decorations at stores all around Kittiport, and what was in the box was only a fraction of everything she had bought. The rest she was planning on putting up at the house that she shared with her grandmother, Ann. Her grandmother's house had a huge yard, and backed up to a state park, so there would be plenty of space for outdoor decorations. Ellie had always loved decorating for each holiday, even the ones that people didn't normally do much for.

Before long, fake leaves and miniature turkeys decorated the tables, and she had set out a box to collect cans of food for the local food drive. She had also put up a couple of posters advertising their Black

Friday sales – the pizzeria wouldn't be open on Thanksgiving Day, of course, but they'd be up bright and early to feed the hordes of shoppers that would appear on the streets the next day.

Ellie was just putting the finishing touches on a turkey decal on the clear glass window of the soda fridge when the front door opened with a jingle. In walked a woman that she had seen only once before; Karen Becker, a psychologist from Benton Harbor, the next town down the coast.

"Oh good, I was hoping you'd be in," Karen said. "Wow. This place really gets into the holidays, huh?"

"I love decorating. I'm already planning what I'm going to do for Christmas, and I've just now put the Thanksgiving stuff up," Ellie admitted. "Is everything okay? Anything I can help you with? Would you like to place an order?"

"I'll see what you have," Karen said. She walked up to the register and gazed at the menu above. "Really I just stopped in to say hi and to see your restaurant. I've got some time off. After what happened, I figured I could use a break."

"You deserve it, after nearly getting killed," Ellie said. "It's nice of you to stop by. If you want, maybe you and I and Shannon could all get coffee together sometime."

"That sounds like it would be nice." The psychologist shot her a smile, which she returned. She still felt bad about leading a killer right into the woman's office. It seemed amazing that Karen would even talk to her after all of that.

"Do you want to try our new brownie bits?" she asked. "We just put them on the menu this weekend. People have been asking for a dessert, and I figured brownies would be pretty hard to mess up, even for a pizza place."

"Sure, I'm always in the mood for chocolate."

Ellie brought out two servings of the brownies and joined Karen at a corner booth. The woman talked for a bit about their shared experience with the madwoman who had held a letter opener to the psychologist's throat, then turned the subject to happier things. Karen, it turned out, had spent a few years in Chicago, first to complete her graduate program to get her doctorate in psychology, then for a few years working at someone else's practice before she moved to Maine to open her own.

The door opened again and another customer walked in, a pretty blond woman who was all smiles. Ellie got up to take her order, then returned to the table.

"But why Benton Harbor?" she asked, resuming their conversation. "I'd imagine somewhere like Portland, or pretty much any city, would supply a lot more clients. Even if you see people from Kittiport, too, well… there just aren't that many people around here."

"I like the small-town feel," Karen said. "And it's true that there aren't that many people, but there also isn't much competition. I keep my prices low, and I see people from all over. Reputation means a lot in my field, and I've had people drive hours to see me just because someone they know recommended my practice."

"Wow. It sounds like you've got a pretty good client base built up," Ellie said.

"You must, as well. I did a search for Papa Pacelli's online, and I saw that this place has been here for almost twenty years. Have you been working here the whole time?"

"No, this place was actually my grandfather's. I only moved here a couple of months ago…" Ellie went on to tell her all about her grandparents, and her own history in Chicago. It was nice talking to someone else who had lived in the Midwest, and who had seen more of the world than just the coast of Maine. She loved everyone she knew in Kittiport, but most of them had spent their entire lives in the same small town. She was beginning to realize that she and Karen had a lot in common. With any luck, they would continue to stay in touch, and possibly even build a friendship out of all the craziness that had happened a few weeks ago.

After the psychologist left, Ellie got back to work on the decorations while Clara and Rose kept the kitchen running and the deliveries going out smoothly. It was satisfying to see how smoothly they all worked together, especially compared to how the pizzeria had been running before she took over, and she was proud of how much they had all improved. She enjoyed coming in to work most days, something that she had rarely if ever felt back in Chicago, and she knew a large part of that had to do with how well everyone who worked at the pizzeria got along. They were beginning to feel something like a family to her.

"Hey, Ms. Pacelli, we're about to make a pizza for lunch," Rose said, poking her head through the door that lead to the kitchen. "What do you want on your part?"

"Chicken and green peppers," Ellie said. "Thanks. I'm about done out here, then I'll come and join you."

Just as she was about to call it a day and pack up the few remaining decorations that she hadn't found a place for, her cell phone buzzed. She reached into her pocket, pulled it out, and checked the caller ID. Russell. She clicked it onto silent and put it back into her pocket, not because she didn't want to talk to him, but because when she did talk to him, she didn't want to be distracted. The two of them had gone on one date, which hadn't exactly been a success due to Ellie's status as the town's pariah at the time, and they had never actually discussed it. She didn't know where exactly their relationship stood at the moment, and didn't think that the middle of her day at the pizzeria was exactly the best time to figure it out.

Oh, well, she thought. *At least everything else is back to normal. Russell and I will have plenty of time to talk now that things have calmed down.* Her mood boosted by the thought of how well the pizzeria had been doing now that the town knew she hadn't been responsible for poisoning anybody, Ellie smiled to herself and headed towards the kitchen, eager to get started on her two slices of what was easily the best pizza for miles around.

CHAPTER TWO

E ven though she had spent the better part of the day before getting Papa Pacelli's ready for Thanksgiving, Ellie was still suffering from the itch to decorate. Planning the meals would come later, of course, but for now she wanted to focus on getting the setting just right – which was turning out to be more difficult than she had expected.

"Calm down, Marlowe," she said as the giant red and green parrot ran past her. The bird could move surprisingly fast when she wanted to, and Ellie usually found the sight of her scurrying along the floor amusing. Not today, though. Marlowe was mad, and when Marlowe was mad, someone usually got bit.

"Bad dog!" the parrot squawked. Her head was tilted to the side and one intense yellow eye was staring straight up at the paper turkey hanging from the ceiling. "Bad dog!"

Those were the bird's new favorite words, which she had taken to yelling at anything she didn't like. She had picked it up one day when Ellie had been admonishing Bunny, her papillon, for getting up on her grandfather's desk and attempting to eat a whole bowl of treats. Soon after, the parrot had discovered that whenever she squawked those two words, Bunny would retreat out of the room with her head down and her tail tucked between her legs. Now, Marlowe seemed to hope the same strategy would work with the turkey that was hanging from the ceiling, but she was having no such luck.

"Bad dog bad dog!"

Seeing the bird getting even more upset, Ellie attempted to pick her up once again, and only narrowly managed to dodge a nip from Marlowe's large beak.

"It's not a real bird, Marlowe," she said, becoming exasperated. "It's just a decoration. Here, I'll take it down, all right?"

She climbed back up on the wobbly ladder and pulled the turkey down. After placing it out of sight on the stairs, Ellie was able to get the bird back in her cage, which she then wheeled to the study. She felt bad about putting the parrot in the other room, but if Marlowe was that scared of one fake bird, she couldn't imagine the bird would be comfortable when her grandmother's friends came over for their annual Thanksgiving dinner. The macaw had never been a fan of guests, and she didn't have any reason to believe that Thanksgiving would be an exception to that policy.

"You'll be fine in here," Ellie told her as she parked the cage in its old spot in the corner by the window. She paused to pull up a playlist of some classical music on her computer so Marlowe would have something to listen to, then left the room to get back to decorating. Shannon Ward, a woman who she had been friends with way back in high school, was coming over soon to help her meal plan, and she wanted to have *something* done by the time the other woman got there.

Ellie spent a few more minutes putting up decorations, after she replaced the offending turkey in the foyer, before she heard a car pull into the driveway. It sounded louder than she expected from her friend's quiet sedan. Peeking out one of the tall windows by the front door, she was surprised to see Russell's truck idling behind her little green car. Her first thought was that something had happened to her grandmother, who was currently out to lunch with one of her friends.

Feeling scared, Ellie opened the front door and approached the truck barefooted. Relief washed over her when she saw Shannon get out of the passenger side. The sheriff must have given her a ride for some reason; he wasn't here to deliver bad news.

"Thank goodness," she breathed. As Shannon approached, Russell gave her a wave goodbye through the windshield, then put his truck into reverse and pulled out of the driveway. Ellie felt a small pang; she wished that he would stay and talk more; they had been laying telephone tag since he called her at the pizzeria. *If he's too busy, it's with good reason,* she told herself. *He's the sheriff, after all.*

"Is everything all right with your car?" she asked her friend as they walked back to the house together.

"It had a flat tire this morning," Shannon told her. "I took it in to the shop, but they were already buried in work for the day, and James had already left to go to his own job, so I had to call Russell to see if he'd give me a ride here. Can you take me back to the auto shop later? I'm sorry, I should have asked sooner, but it's been a crazy morning."

"Of course, it's not a problem at all. I was planning on stopping in at Papa Pacelli's for the last few hours before close anyway, so I can drop you off then."

"Thanks. I don't know why the repair place was so busy this morning. I swear, it's like people are going crazy before the holidays or something."

With Shannon there to help out, the task of decorating the entire house for the holiday went more quickly, and was also a lot more fun. Of course, having someone there to hold the ladder was a bonus, too. Ann Pacelli's house was large, with high ceilings and plenty of places to put knick-knacks.

"Nonna's friends are going to love this," Ellie said as they finished.

"And James says *I* go crazy for decorations," Shannon said, shaking her head with amazement as she took a step back to look at everything they had accomplished.

Shannon was a journalist who had a column in the local paper and had gotten knee-deep into trouble alongside Ellie more than a few times in the past couple of months. The two had rekindled their friendship shortly after the pizzeria manager had returned to her childhood hometown, and now were as close as ever.

"I like having fun with this sort of thing," Ellie said. "Halloween, Thanksgiving, Christmas… even the fourth of July and Valentine's day. I can't wait until after Thanksgiving when I can start putting lights up. This big pine tree Nonna has in the front yard will look *great* decked out in white and blue. And of course, I'll have to find some reindeer or maybe a big snowman to go next to it…"

"Don't get ahead of yourself," Shannon said, laughing. "It's barely November. Just wait for the Christmas parade. I bet you could get a float for the restaurant. It would be great advertising."

"One thing at a time," the pizzeria manager said, laughing. "Right now I need to figure out what exactly I'm doing for Thanksgiving, and after that I need to make sure the house and pizzeria are prepared for winter. With Nonna spending so much time out here alone while I'm in town, we can't be too careful."

CHAPTER THREE

Ellie was glad for the weekend, when it came. She didn't know why, but the pizzeria had been busier each evening. Maybe it was the colder weather, or the fact that it got dark earlier than ever, making people feel less inclined to go out of their way to buy groceries and cook, but whatever it was, it was a mixed blessing. On the one hand, she was glad to see Papa Pacelli's positively bustling with business. On the other, she and her employees were working their fingers down to the bone to keep the pizzas rolling out of the kitchen quickly enough.

They weren't the only ones feeling worn out. Nonna had been acting a lot more tired than usual lately, and her granddaughter was worried about her. The elderly woman was well into her eighties, and thought she at times seemed like an unstoppable force of nature, Ellie knew that her grandmother wouldn't be able to continue at the same pace forever. Despite her waning energy, however, Ann Pacelli refused to settle down. She continued to keep up a healthy social life, and also attended various classes on top of her never-ending doctor appointments.

It didn't come as any surprise to Ellie when Nonna came home that evening after having a dinner with one of her old friends and announced that she was going straight to bed.

"All right," she said to her grandmother. "Let me know if you need anything, okay? Remember, you can just ring the bell at the bottom of the stairs — there's no need to come all the way up. I brought some brownies home from the pizzeria, so if you wake up later, feel free to help yourself to some." She knew the older woman tended to wake up in the middle of the night unable to return to sleep on the evenings that she went to bed so early.

"I'll be fine, Eleanora," Nonna said. "I'm old, I'm not a child."

With that, she vanished into her first-floor bedroom, and Ellie was left to frown after her in silence. The older woman wasn't usually so short with her. *Is she in pain?* she wondered. *Is there something going on that she isn't telling me about?*

Deciding to ask her grandmother about it in the morning, the pizzeria manager finished her bowl of lentil soup and washed the few dishes that were in the sink before calling Bunny over and going upstairs to her own bedroom. It was more of a master suite, really;

she had the entire upper level to herself, mainly because the stairs were a major obstacle to her grandmother these days. She still hadn't done much with the spare rooms — at first, she hadn't been sure how long she was going to stay in Kittiport, and lately there just hadn't been time to do much of anything besides work. She would like to get her own office-type area set up here eventually. She loved her grandfather's study, but it still very much felt like *his* study. It would be nice to have a place that felt more like her own.

I could always move out and rent a house in town. She dismissed the thought immediately. There was no way she could leave the elderly woman alone in this big house, especially not with the way she seemed to be slowing down lately. She may not have been very involved with this side of her family for most of her adult life, but that just meant that she had to try harder than ever to do right by her grandmother while she still had the time to make up for it.

After reading for an hour in the comfortable nook by the window, Ellie went to bed with the thought that she would get up early the next morning and do some online shopping for furniture for the little office she wanted to turn the upstairs guest room into.

She lay her head on the pillow and what felt like only seconds later her eyes blinked open. It was still dark outside. She wondered for a moment if she had even slept at all, but the red digits of the clock on her nightstand assured her that she had. It was just past two in the morning. Groaning, Ellie turned over and pulled the comforter farther up her body, trying to get back to sleep. She was going to be up late the next night, and she knew she would regret it if she didn't get a good night's rest now.

A soft, high-pitched whine made her open her eyes again. Bunny must have to go out; that was probably what woke her up in the first place. With a sigh, she gave up on sleep for the moment, sat up, and slipped her feet into the slippers that she kept beside her bed. Early November in Maine was cold, and the hardwood floors throughout the house were freezing on her bare feet at night.

"Come on," she said, still not feeling fully awake. "Let's go outside." She opened the bedroom door and the little black and white papillon dashed through. Ellie could hear her nails clicking on the floor as she ran through the hall, then down the stairs. She followed the dog more slowly, and covered a yawn with one hand as she unlocked the front door and pulled it open with the other.

"Bunny?" she said, puzzled when the dog didn't dash outside. She looked around, but didn't spot the dog anywhere near her feet. Then she heard another soft whine and turned to see the papillon, her white fur bright in the dark hallway, standing by the door to the basement.

"What're you doing?" Ellie asked. She shut the front door and walked down the hallway. To her shock, the basement door was open. It was always supposed to remain closed; Arthur Pacelli, her grandfather, had placed mouse and rat poison down there for years, and though she had tried to gather as much of it up as she could, she wasn't certain that she had gotten it all. The last thing she wanted was for Bunny to get into it. The dog was so small that it wouldn't take much to poison her. "Stay back from there, Bunny."

She placed her hand on the door, meaning to close it, but paused. Had she heard something from below? She listened. There was a rusting sound. She remembered the string of slashed tires that Russell had told her about and wondered fleetingly if someone had broken into the house. That would be just her luck. She would rather have slashed tires.

She was just about to go find something she could defend herself with if the need arose, when she heard a groan coming from the bottom of the stairs.

"Nonna?" Heart pounding, Ellie reached over and flicked on the basement light. Her grandmother was lying at the bottom of the stairs, clutching her left arm to her chest, eyes tightly shut against the pain.

The minutes between her call to 911 and the ambulance's arrival were the longest of Ellie's life. She sat in the basement with her grandmother, afraid to move the older woman, afraid that she would somehow hurt her even more than she had already been.

When she finally heard the ambulance arrive, she hurried up the stairs and locked Bunny in the study so the little dog would be safely out of the way, then opened the front door as the paramedics hurried in. Everything seemed to be happening in jerks and flashes, and before she knew it she was in her car behind the ambulance with no real memory of how she had got there.

Ellie waited at the hospital for hours, occasionally feeling like she should call someone and let them know what had happened, but realizing that they didn't actually have any other family in the area. She didn't know how to get into contact with any of her grandmother's friends. It didn't make sense to call Darlene, her cousin, until she knew more. She lived out of state, and wouldn't be able to do anything other than worry anyway.

At long last the doctor came into the waiting room and settled down in the chair next to her. Ellie searched his face, wondering if the news she was about to hear would be the worst news of her life.

"Your grandmother will be fine," he said. Relief washed over her. "She has a broken arm, and a few bruises that are going to make life pretty miserable for the next few days, but no internal injuries or damage to her head or spine that we've been able to find. I know it may not seem like it now, but she got lucky. She's still out from the surgery on her arm, but you can go and see her if you'd like."

Ellie followed him down the hall, not paying any attention to the turn that he took, until they reached her grandmother's room. Now that she knew Nonna would be okay, she realized that there were still so many questions that she didn't have the answer to, such as why the elderly woman had been going into the basement in the middle of the night in the first place. For now, however, she was content to sit by her grandmother's bed and hold her hand, thinking about how she was going to buy Bunny a box of her favorite treats on her way home.

CHAPTER FOUR

The house seemed empty and lifeless without the elderly woman puttering around the rooms. Ellie was so used to her grandmother's presence that it felt odd to be the only one there, even though she had spent years living on her own. The doctor had told her that Ann would be able to come home in a few days, but he wanted to keep her over the weekend to make sure no additional problems presented themselves.

"A woman her age, it's amazing she survived a fall like that. I've seen other people break a hip or get a concussion after they trip and fall on the carpet," he had told her.

Somehow the prospect of a weekend of relaxing at home didn't seem like such an attractive idea any more. It wasn't like sitting around the big empty house would do anything to help her grandmother, anyway, and she doubted she'd be able to relax in the slightest. She decided that going into the pizzeria would be the best way to get her mind off of Nonna's fall. Keeping busy had always served her best when she was upset.

Heading into the pizzeria on her day off turned out to be a blessing in disguise. Clara, who rarely took time off if she could help it, nearly collapsed with relief when she saw her boss walk into the kitchen.

"Thank goodness. I didn't want to call and interrupt you if you were busy doing something, but my stomach is killing me. I think I might have the flu. Can I leave early?"

Ellie took one look at her pale, slightly sweaty employee and nodded. "Definitely. Don't even finish up that pizza. We can't have someone sick around the food. You go home and get some rest. I hope you feel better soon."

"Thanks, Ms. Pacelli," she said. "I'll make it up some time, I promise."

"Don't worry about it."

The truth was, this was exactly what Ellie had wanted. Not for the young woman to be sick, but to have an excuse to bury herself in her work and push her fears and concerns to the side for the rest of the evening.

With Jacob handling the deliveries, Ellie was alone more often than not at Papa Pacelli's that evening. With the light outside quickly fading and the temperature dropping low enough that she was comfortable in the hot kitchen for once, fewer and fewer people were coming in to pick up pizzas. She envied all of the families who were sitting happily at home, waiting for Jacob to knock on their door with dinner. She should be doing the same at home with Nonna. Her heart ached of the proud, kind older woman all alone at the hospital.

She'll be home tomorrow, or Tuesday at the latest, she thought as she smoothed red sauce across the pizza in front of her. *She wouldn't want me to feel bad for her. I should be focusing on the positives. I have a lot to be thankful for. I shouldn't be spending my time moping around. I should try to be more positive* She knew that Nonna had gotten very lucky when she fell down the stairs. The doctor had made it clear that her injuries easily could have been much worse.

It was near to closing time when she got a text from Shannon. Her friend wanted to know if she was at the pizzeria, and if so, whether it was too late to order something for dinner.

Not too late at all, Ellie texted back. *What do you want?*

After reading her friend's reply, she put away the rag she had been using to clean the burners on the stove and set to work making the veggie supreme pizza her friend had requested. Jacob returned a few minutes later from his last delivery of the evening and gave the pizza dough in her hands a cautious look.

"A last-minute call came in?" he guessed.

"Yes, but it was Shannon, and she's going to pick it up," she told him. "You're free to go."

"Thanks, Ms. P."

Smiling at his obvious relief, Ellie got back to work. At the last minute, she decided to put a personal pizza in the oven for herself, too. Without Nonna at home, there was no reason to cook a full meal for dinner when she got back, not when she had a perfectly good kitchen here.

Shannon got there a few minutes before her pizza was done cooking, so Ellie pulled them both a cup of coffee – it had been brewed that morning, but still tasted okay – and joined her friend at one of the tables.

"How's Ann?" Shannon asked.

"She's on a lot of pain medication, so she wasn't very coherent the last time I spoke with her. They're going to begin lessening the dosage this evening and see how she does. I'll just be glad when she's back home."

"If I send her flowers, should they go to the hospital or your place?"

"Send them to the house," Ellie said. "The doctor thinks she'll be able to come home tomorrow afternoon, as long as nothing else comes up."

"I'll call in the morning, so she'll have bouquet waiting for her when she gets back," Shannon said. "Does Russell know about all of this?"

"Yes, but we, ah, haven't really had a chance to talk lately. I think he's mad at me." He had called her just a few hours ago, but she had been in the middle of a discussion with one of her regulars, and when she had tried to return his call, he hadn't answered.

"Mad at you?" Her friend laughed. "Why in the world do you think that?"

"He's been more distant since the mayor's wife died and everything happened with Karen," Ellie said. "I think he's upset that I didn't listen to his warnings and ended us all up in a bucket full of trouble."

To her surprise, Shannon chuckled and shook her head. "He's not mad at you, Ellie. From what James had told me, he's mad at himself for not listening to what you were trying to tell him. He blames himself for me, you, and Karen being in that situation."

"Well, that's stupid of him," Ellie said bluntly. "I'm the one that dragged us into the mess."

"That's not how he sees it. You know about his wife. He's never forgiven himself for not finding her killer. I think he probably feels like your near brush with death is his fault too."

"It wasn't exactly a near brush with death. I mean, Karen was the only one that was in immediate danger."

"Still." Shannon shrugged. "I'm just guessing that's how he feels. He's the kind of guy that thinks everything is his responsibility, even when it isn't. A few years ago, James got into a car accident involving a deer, and he was beating himself up because he was the one that had suggested that James take that route to avoid traffic. James even admitted that he had been sending me a text when he hit the deer, and Russell still blames himself."

"So what should I do?"

"Just talk to him," Shannon said. "Ignore all of his weird, manly feelings of guilt and show him that you're completely fine."

"I'll give that a try. Hold on, that's the oven. Your pizza's done."

Shannon followed her back into the pizzeria's kitchen and rinsed out her coffee cup in the sink while Ellie took the pizza out of the oven and slid it into a box for her friend. She was just reaching back into the oven for her mini pizza when she heard the bell that signified someone had opened the front door.

"I'll go tell whoever it is that you're closed. Do you want me to turn off the sign, too?"

"Sure. Thanks," Ellie said.

She put her own pizza on top of the stove and was just beginning to fold one of the eight inch boxes when she heard an earsplitting scream come from the dining area. Dropping the box, Ellie ran across the kitchen and pushed her way through the swinging door to find Shannon standing frozen behind the counter with her hands covering her mouth. On the floor in the middle of the pizzeria was a blonde woman, who was lying crumpled in a growing pool of blood. The front door was still closing, and Ellie caught a glimpse of someone dressed all in black run down the sidewalk outside.

CHAPTER FIVE

Ellie hurried forward to help the woman on the ground. Behind her, she could hear the Shannon's phone beeping as she dialed, presumably calling 911. She fell to her knees next to the woman, her hands fluttering uselessly above the still form, feeling just as helpless as she had when she was waiting for the ambulance to come and get her grandmother from the bottom of the basement stairs.

Focus, she told herself, straining to remember everything she knew about first aide. It wasn't much, but she thought that stopping the bleeding was probably the first thing she could do.

She pressed her hands against the wound on the woman's back, trying not to recoil at the warm, wet touch of her blood. Pressing down on the only wound she could see, she tried to staunch the flow. The woman didn't gasp or twitch even slightly as she applied pressure, which Ellie knew couldn't possibly be a good sign. Faintly, as if from far away, she heard Shannon's panicked voice saying something to the emergency operator, but she was too focused on the blond woman to pay attention to what was being said. The woman still struck her as looking familiar. She gazed at her face for a long moment before realizing who she was; the woman who had come in to pick up a pizza earlier in the week while she was having lunch with Karen. She wished she could remember her name — it had been something unique, she was sure of it. That was why the woman's face had stuck with her.

"Just hold on," she said softly. "Help is on the way." She didn't know if the woman could hear her or not. She didn't appear to be breathing, but Ellie was to scared of taking the pressure from her wound to take the time to check her pulse.

After what felt like an hour, but could have only been minutes, she saw the flashing of lights through the display window as an ambulance pulled up alongside the entrance. She heard the keening of sirens, and hoped the police were on their way too.

She moved aside as the paramedics ran up and began checking the woman for signs of life as they moved her onto an emergency stretcher. Shannon came up behind her and put a hand on her shoulder, and the two of them watched mutely as the woman was rolled away. She hadn't moved at all since Ellie had first knelt behind her, and when she saw the open, unseeing eyes, she knew that despite her best efforts, the woman hadn't made it.

Russell walked through the door just after the paramedics left. He paused halfway in and followed their progress to the ambulance with his gaze, his eyes sad. Liam flanked him, his eyes going from the pool of blood on the trail to Ellie's bloodstained hands, but he didn't say anything, waiting instead for his sheriff to speak.

Russell seemed to pale when he saw Shannon and Ellie standing side by side, one of them covered in blood, and the other shaking like a leaf. "Are both of you all right?" They nodded. He took a deep breath, then unclipped his walkie talkie from his belt and spoke into it.

"Bethany, tell my brother that his wife is all right. She's here with Eleanora and they both appear to be unharmed. You can let him come on in." He turned to the two women and beckoned them over. "I'll need a statement from each of you, but first you two should get cleaned up. James is waiting on the other side of the police barricade. I'm sure he'll want to go to the station with you. I'll be over there as soon as I get everything under control here."

"Do you think you'll be able to find the killer?" Ellie asked.

"Doubtful," Russell said. "We'll look, of course, but even if he or she hung around after attacking the victim, then I'm sure they took off when they saw the police vehicles pull up. Did you see anything that might help us identify the killer?"

"No, sorry," she said. "They were dressed completely in black, but that's all I saw."

"I think it was a man," Shannon said. Her voice was quiet, and her eyes were wet. "She kicked him when he attacked her, and the grunt he made sounded like a man's voice. And he wasn't much taller than her."

"That helps," he said. "Thanks, Shannon."

Russell pulled a worn looking notebook out of his jacket pocket and scribbled in it. Ellie knew it was a pitifully short list that he was writing down. *Maybe they'll be able to get prints from the knife*, she thought hopefully.

He looked up from his note pad as a handsome man pushed his way through the door. "I'm so glad you're all right," he said, his eyes glued to his wife.

"James," Shannon hugged him tightly, then pulled back to look up at his face. "How did you hear about this?"

"Russell called me as soon as he got the call about an attack at the pizzeria. When he told me you were the one that made the call…" He closed his eyes and shook his head. "I thought you might have been the one that got hurt, too."

"I'm fine, James. Ellie's fine too."

"Good. Are you two free to go?"

"I need to take an official statement from them first. I was going to have Bethany take them down to the station, unless you want to drive them, and they can get cleaned up and calm down a bit and see if they remember anything else."

"Can't you take their statements tomorrow?" James asked.

"They witnessed a murder. I need the information as soon as possible."

"Russ, this is my wife we're talking about. Let me take her home. It's not like either of them killed the lady. Whatever information you need, they're not going to forget it between now and tomorrow morning."

"Would you quit talking about us like we aren't here?" Shannon said, pulling away from her husband. "I, for one, would rather get it over with now."

"Me too," Ellie said. "I think talking about it will help."

"Fine." James ran his fingers through his hair. "Women. I'm going to go grey because of you."

James ended up driving them to the sheriff's department, freeing Bethany to help with the search for the killer. After Ellie scrubbed her hands clean, she and Shannon were lead to a comfortable interview room, where they each given a cup of coffee and asked to wait. It didn't take long for Russell to return from the crime scene. He interviewed them separately, going over the attack again, but also asking other questions about the evening and the woman who had been attacked. He seemed surprised when Ellie said that she had recognized her.

"Papa Pacelli's is a popular restaurant," he said. "How come you remembered her specifically?"

"She used her card to pay. I remember thinking how much I liked her name. It was something unique, and very pretty... Celestine, that was it."

He nodded. "Had you ever seen her before that day? Had she ordered pizzas previously?"

"Possibly. I could check the records at the pizzeria. If she paid with her card previously, then it would show up. Why?"

"She wasn't a local," he said. "At least, not according to her driver's license. But she had some receipts in her wallet from local stores with dates spanning the past couple of months. If she ever ordered a pizza for delivery, that might tell us where she's staying."

"I'll check first thing tomorrow," Ellie promised.

"Thanks." He stood up and indicated that she should do the same. "I think that's all I need for now. Do you need a ride home?"

"Just back to the pizzeria. My car's there."

"All right, I'll take you there. I'm glad you're okay, Ellie. I'm sorry you keep getting dragged into this sort of thing. Be careful, all right?"

"I always am."

CHAPTER SIX

Ellie woke up the next morning feeling as if she hadn't slept at all. Whenever she closed her eyes, scenes from the murder flashed through her brain. She kept wondering if there was anything she could have done differently, and kept kicking herself for not knowing more about first aid. Twice in the past week she had failed to do anything other than call an ambulance when someone needed help. Maybe she should have applied pressure differently, or tried to keep the woman awake. Part of her wanted to look it up online, but the rational part of her mind told her that would be a bad idea. If she found out that there *had* been something else she could have done to try to save the woman, she would never forgive herself.

At least she had one thing to look forward to today to take her mind off the murder; Nonna was coming home. Ellie was supposed to pick her up at noon, which gave her a few hours to make sure the house was clean and throw some cookies or muffins into the oven.

She was determined to make her grandmother's homecoming perfect. She may have only been gone for the weekend, but it felt like a lot longer.

"There you go," Ellie said as she buckled the elderly woman into the passenger side seat of her car. "I've got your medicine in my purse, and your doctor's number in my phone."

"Thanks for picking me up, dear," Ann said. "I hope it wasn't too much trouble for you."

"Trouble? Not at all, Nonna. I missed you. It'll be good to have you back."

She hadn't told her grandmother about the murder at the pizzeria yet, though she knew she couldn't keep it secret forever. The elderly woman didn't need any more stress in her life, though; as far as Ellie was concerned, all Ann Pacelli should focus on was healing her broken bones and recovering from her fall.

The drive back from the hospital took nearly half an hour, and by the time they returned to the Pacelli house, Nonna had fallen asleep. Ellie had no choice but to prod her gently awake and help her hobble inside. Her phone rang, but she ignored it. Bunny greeted them at the door and even though she was almost vibrating with excitement, she seemed to sense that jumping up on the older woman wouldn't be a good idea. Instead, the papillon ran circles around their feet as the two women made their slow way down the hall to Nonna's room.

"It feels good to be back," the elderly woman said, seeming to perk up a bit as she took in the familiar surroundings. "And it smells simply amazing. Are you baking something?"

"Cranberry orange muffins," Ellie said. "I made them fresh right before I left to get you. Would you like some?"

"Yes, that would be lovely. And a cup of tea if you will, sweetie. Chamomile."

A few minutes later Ellie returned to the bedroom with a tray laden with muffins and tea for two. She sat on the edge of the bed and took her cup of tea before handing the tray over to her grandmother.

"So tell me, Nonna, what happened? Why were you going into the basement in the middle of the night?"

"I didn't mean to," Ann said. "I must have gotten confused. I went to bed so early that I woke up in the middle of the night having to use the toilet. I must have opened the wrong door. I remember falling, but not much else. Thank goodness you found me before morning."

"I wouldn't have if Bunny hadn't woken me up," Ellie said. She felt a surge of affection for the little dog, and reached down to help her up onto the bed. "She's really the one that saved you. She must have heard you fall."

"What a good girl." The elderly woman patted the dog gently with her good hand.

"Nonna, we should talk about what happens if you fall and I'm not here," Ellie said. "Maybe we should get you some sort of panic button."

"I don't want a panic button."

"But what if you fall sometime while I'm at work and you can't get up? You could by lying there for hours."

"I just won't walk around the house in the dark again. I'll be fine, Ellie. This was an accident. I'm perfectly capable of taking care of myself."

Ellie pursed her lips but didn't push it. She could sense that this would be an ongoing argument, but now wasn't the time to get into it.

"How's your tea?"

"Just perfect, dear. Thank you."

Once they had finished their tea and muffins, she left the room, shutting the door quietly behind her and hoping her grandmother would get some rest. She had been planning on going in to the pizzeria for the last few hours just to help out – it was opening late today, anyway, while the police finished up their investigation – but was toying with the idea of calling the restaurant and seeing if her employees would be okay without her. It didn't seem right to leave her nonna alone so soon after she had gotten out of the hospital. *No,* she thought, *I can't do that. I promised Russell that I'd check the records and see if Celestine had ever ordered a delivery pizza. I've got to go in for that, at least. Besides, who knows what might happen once people realize someone was killed in the restaurant.*

Suddenly she remembered the call that she had missed. She fumbled for her phone, hoping against hope that it had been the sheriff calling to tell her that the killer had been caught. But no, her caller ID said that Jacob had been the one to call. Sighing, she dialed his number.

"Hey Ms. Pacelli, it's all right, Iris covered for me," he said when he answered.

"What are you talking about?" she asked.

"Didn't you get my message?"

"Sorry, I didn't listen to it. What's going on?"

"Well, someone slashed my tires and I had to call a tow truck just to get out of my driveway. I should still be able to make it to my shift on Wednesday, though."

"Iris took your shift?"

"Right."

"Okay. Thanks for letting me know. Sorry I didn't answer."

"It's fine, Ms. P. See ya Wednesday."

He hung up. Ellie frowned at her phone for a moment before putting it back in her pocket. First Shannon, and now Jacob had gotten suspicious flats. What was coming over this town?

After making sure her grandmother was sleeping peacefully, Ellie left the house and made her way towards town. Jacob was out of commission until his car got fixed, and Clara was out of town for the next few days, so that didn't leave them any extra employees. She doubted that Rose and Iris would be able to handle the pizzeria themselves that evening since it was likely to be busier than usual due to the holidays, and Iris was still learning her way around the kitchen. That meant that she had no choice but to go in and help out for the rest of the evening, whether or not she was able to get the information for Russell.

As she drove through town, she noticed that Kittiport had gone through an amazing transformation over the last few days. With everything that had been going on over the last twenty-four hours, it had been easy for her to forget about the approaching holidays, but the rest of the town hadn't forgotten. All month previously, it had looked as if a Halloween decoration factory had exploded in town, but now every spooky decoration was gone, a few trees had already been dressed up with soft white and blue lights, and Black Friday sale signs dominated the display windows of nearly every store.

The biggest retail day of the year was drawing ever closer, and for the first time, Ellie felt the stirring of anticipation, not as a consumer, but as someone who was hoping to make a lot of sales that day. Nearly everyone in town would be out shopping the Friday after Thanksgiving. She just hoped that shopping made them hungry, because the pizzeria would be more than happy to feed them all.

CHAPTER SEVEN

T he first thing Ellie did when she got to the pizzeria was print off the order records for the past two months. She poured herself a cup of soda from the open two-liter in the employee fridge and settled herself down at the table in the kitchen to pour over the papers. It was slow going. More people tended to pay with credit cards than with cash, and the pizzeria had been busier than ever the past couple of months. When she finally found the name that she was looking for, she exclaimed, causing Iris to jump in surprise.

"What's going on?"

"Nothing, sorry," Ellie said.

She underlined the entry and felt a stab of disappointment. It had been another pickup order. With a sigh, she took a sip of her soda and kept going down the list.

Near the end of the last page, she saw Celestine's name again. She underlined it and followed the entry across the page with her pen. It was a delivery. Grinning, she wrote the address down on the back of the paper and took a picture of it with her cell phone, which she then sent to Russell in a text message, along with the date and time of the order. Feeling triumphant, she stacked the papers neatly and was about to stand up and get to work for real when she noticed something. When she had first sat down to look at the papers, she had started from the date that Celestine had come in to the pizzeria earlier that week, which meant that she hadn't even looked at the more recent orders. Near the top of the first page was Celestine's name again, and it was another delivery. She had ordered a pizza the day before she had died.

"What do you think it means?"

"I have no idea," Ellie said. She stirred her butternut squash soup and blew on a spoonful tentatively before tasting it. Perfect. "I told Russell about it, of course. Jacob was the one that delivered it to her, so I imagine that he'll have to go in for questioning at some point."

"You don't think it could have been him, do you?" Shannon asked, her eyes going wide. It was the Wednesday after her grandmother had returned home, and they were eating lunch at a small bistro a couple of blocks away from the pizzeria. Karen was with them, listening with interest as she sipped a triple caramel hot chocolate.

"No, of course not," Ellie said. "But he may have seen someone else there with her, and it's possible that that person could be the killer. I haven't had much of a chance to talk to Russell — I don't know if he'd tell me anything else anyway — but from what he's said, this lady isn't a local, but she's been in town for at least a month. He needed the address from the delivery to figure out where she was staying."

"Well, what's the address?" her friend asked.

Ellie recited it. "I already drove by, just out of curiosity. It's some old house between here and Benton Harbor. I've got no idea who lives there."

"So we have a mysterious woman killed by an even more mysterious person dressed all in black," Shannon mused. "Where's she from?"

"No idea. Russell didn't mention it, and I didn't think to ask."

"Why does it matter?" Karen asked. Both women turned to look at her. "Well, I mean, it's the job of the police to figure all of this stuff out, isn't it?"

"Yeah," Ellie said. "But I'm still curious. I guess I feel connected to her, somehow. I had her blood on my hands…" She looked down at her fingers and shivered. She would never forget how it had felt to try so desperately to save someone's life, and fail.

"There's nothing wrong with being proactive," Shannon said. "The case does effect both of us."

"What do you mean?"

"Well, the killer saw both of us, didn't he?" her friend said. "What if he wants to get rid of the witnesses?"

Ellie blinked. She hadn't thought of that. Her interest in the case had been nothing but a morbid sort of curiosity up until now, but Shannon had a point. The two of them had been the only ones to see the murder happen.

"I don't know," she said slowly. "It's not like we can identify him. You said yourself that he was wearing a ski mask and you couldn't see anything to identify him. Killing more people would just make it more likely that he's get caught, wouldn't it?"

"Well, yeah, but this person stabbed a lady in the middle of your store. He's not exactly a rational thinker. Someone who was that worried about getting caught wouldn't have committed a murder in the first place."

"He may not have gotten more than a glance at either of us. What are the chances he would know who we are?"

"Well, it's your family's store, for one. He probably didn't see you, though – he was already on his way out the door when you came in. But I was just standing out in the open. There's no way he didn't get a good look at me."

Ellie realized that her friend was right. If the killer was a local, there was every chance that he could have recognized her. Shannon wrote for the local paper, and her picture had been in the paper a few times.

"You two lead exciting lives," Karen said into the silence, looking between them. "And I don't mean that as a compliment."

"You just met us at a bad time," Shannon said. "Life around here is usually pretty quiet."

"Just don't go leading any more killers into my office, okay?"

"We'll do our best."

They kept the conversation away from the murder for the rest of their meal, though Shannon still seemed distracted. Ellie was worried about her; if her friend was right and the killer *had* recognized her, then she could very well be in danger.

The women were just standing up to leave when something happened that made all three of them jump. Another patron, a large, balding man, leapt out of his seat and shouted "Hey, that's my car!"

He was looking out the window, and Ellie turned reflexively to follow his gaze just as the car's alarm went off. She caught a glimpse of someone running away from a red sports car that now boasted a broken rear window and what looked like two flat tires.

"I wonder if that's the same person that did my car," Shannon muttered as the balding man ran outside and looked around for the vandal.

"Someone slashed Jacob's tires, too," Ellie said. "What in the world has come over this town?"

CHAPTER EIGHT

J acob was eager to tell his story at work the next day; not only had someone slashed his tires on Monday, but he had also been questioned by the sheriff. It had been an exciting week for the young man. After her conversation with Shannon at the bistro the day before, Ellie was more eager than ever to hear good news about the case. She hovered behind her employee as clocked in and began pelting him with questions.

"What all did the sheriff ask you?"

"Just, like, if I'd seen anyone else there, and if she seemed worried about anything."

"Well, did she? *Was* anyone else there?"

"She didn't seem worried, and yeah, there was someone else there. I heard a guy's voice. I didn't see him, though."

Ellie bit her lower lip and tried to think. It didn't seem like Russell had gotten anything useful from Jacob, which meant that he probably wasn't any closer to solving the case. Before her lunch with Shannon and Karen, she had wanted the case solved on behalf of the woman who died, but now it felt more personal. She didn't like the thought of Shannon being in danger. If only she had been the one to go out and tell the woman the pizzeria was closed, then at least her friend wouldn't have to worry about all of this.

"She actually seemed really happy," Jacob went on. "I can't believe she was killed just a day later."

"I know," Ellie said, brought back to the present. "It's terrible. I wish I had been able to do more to help her at the end."

"Well, at least she wasn't alone when she, you know… passed."

The pizzeria manager nodded slowly. She knew she would never forget sitting with the woman for the last moments of her life. It was something that would haunt her forever. Suddenly she wanted to change the subject.

"So, how's your car doing?" she asked, reaching into the fridge for dough. Their first order of the day was their new special; a thin crust pizza with smoked Gouda sauce, caramelized onions, spinach, and garlic. She was convinced that it was one of the best pizzas to ever pass through their doors, and was very impressed with Iris, the newest employee, for coming up with it. She was even considering making it a permanent addition to their menu.

"It's fine, now. I had to get four new tires though. I'm glad we got paid Monday."

"Do you have any idea who did it?" Ellie asked.

"No clue," Jacob said with a shrug. "Probably just some random person, right? I mean, it wasn't a very well-lit part of town. That sort of thing just happens sometimes, doesn't it?"

"I suppose," Ellie said. "Though Kittiport doesn't seem like quite the setting for that sort of vandalism."
Just because it's a small town, doesn't mean everyone's a good person, she reminded herself. *Just look at what happened to Celestine.*

They worked in silence for a while, Ellie putting together the smoked Gouda pizza while Jacob made a new batch of dough. Even with the addition of Iris, she sometimes felt like the staff at the pizzeria was stretched too thinly, especially with Clara out of town until the end of the week and Iris not being fully trained yet. *I could hire someone else in addition to Iris*, she thought. *But that might not give everybody enough hours.* Right now, the hours were split pretty evenly between her employees, with everyone getting two days off a week. If she added someone else to the mix and still tried to keep the hours as even as possible, that would mean smaller paychecks for the whole crew.

Since none of her employees had complained about how busy they were, she thought she would let it be for now. If they were happy and the pizzeria was running smoothly, she saw no reason to change anything. Besides, she was sure Nonna would insist on continuing to help out once she was fully healed from her broken arm. The older woman was doing well — almost too well, in fact — and kept pushing the limits of what Ellie felt she could safely do.

I went from having to take care of only myself and Bunny, to being responsible for my grandmother, a macaw, and four employees, she thought as she pulled the pizza out of the oven. It really was amazing how different her life here was than her life in Chicago. The amazing thing was, was that she was so much happier here even though none of this was a part of her life plan. She hadn't been miserable, exactly, back in Chicago, but she had never once felt the deep peace that she felt here in Kittiport.

She got the smoked Gouda pizza into a box and handed it over to Jacob for delivery. He slid it into an insulated bag and grabbed his keys off the counter, pausing to check the order receipt before leaving.

"Right. See ya in a bit, Ms. Pacelli."

With that he was gone. Iris would be coming in later, but for now Ellie was alone in the pizzeria. It was a nice feeling. She turned up the radio's volume a couple of notches and got to work on the next order; a chicken and broccoli pizza with white sauce.

Once the chicken pizza was out of the oven, Ellie set it on the warming rack and went out front to keep an eye on the register. She browsed the internet on her phone, feeling a bit guilty with the knowledge that she had asked her employees to refrain from doing the same while they were working. Still, no one was there, there wasn't any cleaning that needed to be done and besides, she was the boss.

The bell over the door jingled and she looked up. Two men had walked in, one slightly taller than the other. He had dark hair, and the shorter one was blond, but the build of their faces looked similar. They were deep in conversation, but tapered off into silence as they drew nearer the register.

"Welcome to Papa Pacelli's," she said. "How can I help you?"

"We're picking a pizza up," the taller of the two men said. "It should be under Christopher Gaines."

"The chicken and broccoli?"

"Yep."

"Great. I'll go and get that for you."

She slid off the stool and pushed through the swinging door to the kitchen, turning the volume down on the radio as she walked by. The pizza was toasty warm when she grabbed it off the rack. She double checked the receipt, then walked back out to the front. The two men had resumed their conversation, and barely glanced up when she reappeared.

"Thanks for this, man," the shorter of the two was saying. "I know it might seem weird, but this was her favorite pizza. I feel like we're honoring her memory by getting it. Today would have been our six-month anniversary."

"No problem. I know how you're feeling. It still doesn't seem real that she's gone."

Ellie made a connection between the pizza in her hands and the men's words. She was almost certain that Celestine had ordered a chicken pizza that day she had come in while Karen was there. Her mouth opened before her brain fully registered what she was doing.

"Are you talking about the girl that was murdered on Sunday?" she asked. "Celestine?"

Both men stared at her in surprise. "Yeah," the taller of the two said at last. "Why? Did you know her?"

"I remember her from when she stopped in a while ago," Ellie said. "Not just that, though, I was also the one that sat with her after she was attacked."

The shorter of the two took a step backwards, his eyes going wide. "Wait, are you saying... did you see the person who killed her?"

She nodded.

"Who was it? Did you see their face? Did she seem to know him?" He stepped forward to grip the counter for balance, his face as white as a sheet now. "Who killed my Celestine?"

"Alex," the taller of the two men said, reaching for his friend's shoulder. "Calm down. Don't scare the poor lady."

"Get off me, Chris. I need to know if she saw who killed Celestine. I've got to know. You don't understand, you've never lost someone like her."

His friend backed off, looking hurt. "Just don't scare her, man."

"It's all right," Ellie said, somewhat shaken. "I'm sorry, but whoever attacked her was wearing a mask. I've got no idea who it was, and I've already told everything I know to the police. How did you know her?"

"She was my girlfriend," Alex said, looking pained. "More than that. She was the love of my life. We were going to get married."

Chris made a sound, but covered it up with a cough when Alex glanced back at him.

"Okay, so we had our problems," he admitted, turning back to Ellie. "But we were working on them. If I ever find out who killed her…" He trailed off, frowning angrily and looking down at the counter. Chris cleared his throat and stepped forward.

"I think we'd better pay for that pizza and go," he said. "My little bro's not exactly in a social mood, as you can see."

"Right, sorry," Ellie said. "I didn't mean to bring it up. I'm very sorry for your loss."

She took their money and handed the pizza over, her mind working overtime as she watched the two brothers go.

CHAPTER NINE

Ellie decided that Russell should probably hear about her conversation with the two brothers who had known Celestine. She could just call him, she knew, but it had been a while since she'd seen him and now that he was working on this new case, he would be even busier than usual until it was solved or the trail went cold. The sheriff's department wasn't far from the pizzeria, anyway, and she could easily stop there after closing. She would grab some coffee for them both on the way — the brew at the sheriff's department always seemed to have a slightly burnt taste, no matter how recently it had been made.

She refrained from saying anything to Jacob or Iris when she got there about the brothers. She knew how quickly word could spread in such a small town, and she didn't want to be responsible for starting any gossip about Celestine or her boyfriend. She couldn't imagine how hard it must be on Alex to have lost someone that he so obviously cared deeply about. It just made her feel even worse about her failure to help the woman, and she felt a strong surge of anger towards whoever had killed Celestine.

It was long since dark by the time the pizzeria closed for the day. Ellie locked up and waved goodbye to her employees as they got into their vehicles and drove away. It was another unseasonably warm evening, and for a moment she considered walking over to the sheriff's department. Then she remembered exactly why she was going over there, and realized just how stupid that would be of her to do. *Walking alone through town at night after having witnessed a murder, and with the killer still on the loose*, she thought, shaking her head. *Is something wrong with my instinct of self-preservation?*

She buckled herself into her car and drove the short distance to the coffee shop, where she ordered a pumpkin spice latte for herself, and a double mocha espresso for Russell. She didn't know him well enough to be able to guess his favorite flavor right off the bat, but somehow she didn't see him as a pumpkin spice sort of guy. Mocha seemed like a safe choice, and she already knew how much he loved his caffeine.

She started her car up again and made the second short hop over to the sheriff's department. A drink in each hand, she pushed the door open with her hip and walked inside. There was a new secretary at the desk. Well, new to Ellie. The woman looked to be nearly as old Nonna.

"Can I help you?" she asked, peering over the rim of her glasses, the lenses of which were as thick as the bottom of a beer bottle.

"Um, yes, I'm here to see Sheriff Ward."

"Name?"

"Ellie. Eleanora Pacelli."

"Pacelli, Pacelli..." The woman pushed the glasses farther up her nose and squinted at the computer. "Did he ask you to come in, dear?"

"No, I'm a friend of his. I'm just dropping by." She raised the coffees in her hands. "I brought him a mocha."

"Okay, well you'll have to wait. He's talking to someone else right now."

Feeling a bit put out, Ellie went to go sit down in the uncomfortable plastic chairs. She put the coffees down and picked up a magazine that was nearly a year out of date. She looked at the golden-brown turkey on the cover, and wondered vaguely if there was any way to put turkey on a pizza without making it look like Papa Pacelli's was trying too hard. She loved Thanksgiving as much as the next person, but turkey, stuffing, and cranberry sauce didn't generally make people think of pizzas.

The door across the room opened and she looked up. A gaggle of young women was being ushered through by Russell, who looked tired. The woman in front looked sad, but the other two were talking animatedly, almost angrily.

"I can't believe you're going to let that creep get away with it," one of them was saying. "You should go out and arrest him right now."

"She *told* us that she was going to leave him, and now she's dead. What do you think happened?" the other said. "I don't understand why he's not in jail already. Does anyone at this police station actually *do* anything?"

"I'm going to have to ask you ladies to leave," Russell said. "Thank you very much for the information. I assure you we're doing everything we can to find the person responsible for your friend's death."

He ushered them towards the exit. When his eyes landed on Ellie, relief flashed through them.

"But sheriff —"

"Sorry, ma'am, I have someone else here to see me. I promise, we're doing everything we can."

He gestured Ellie over and left the women gathered in a semi-circle around the secretary's desk. She followed him back through the door that led to the rest of the sheriff's department, shooting a glance over her shoulder at the older woman who was listening patiently as one of the three ladies spoke to her.

"Do you think they're going to leave?" she asked. "It looks like they're just standing there bothering that old woman."

"Mrs. Laffere?" He snorted. "That's Liam's mother. She's filling in for our usual lady. She can handle herself just fine. She worked here for the old sheriff. In fact, I'm pretty sure she's been doing this job since before I could talk."

"Ah. She seems... nice."

"I think she gets a bit confused these days," he said. "But she does a fine job of asking people to wait and paging whoever they're here for, and that's really all we need. Anyway, what's the occasion?" He glanced at the coffees in her hands. "Is one of those for me?"

She nodded. "I got you a mocha espresso." She handed it over. "This is partially a social visit, but mostly I wanted to talk to you about some people who stopped in the pizzeria today…"

She told him about her encounter with the two brothers as they drank their coffee. Russell's forehead creased as he considered what she told him.

"You know, oddly enough, this man, Alex Gaines, is the same person that those women were telling me about."

"Really? They didn't seem to like him very much."

"No, definitely not," Russell said. "What was your impression of him?"

"Well, he seemed nice, I guess. Mostly he just acted sad. And he was very interested when I told him that I'd witnessed her murder."

"I wish you hadn't done that," he said, sounding exasperated. "If he did have anything to do with her death, you very well could be in danger."

"I know." Ellie sighed. She had been thinking about that all day. "I'll just be extra careful now. I'm glad Nonna's back in the house.

She may not be much help if someone broke in, but at least it's better than being completely alone all the way out there."

"How is she doing?" he asked.

"Much better. In a way, she's almost doing too well. She's not being careful at all, and her balance is *worse* now than it was before she fell, since her arm is in a cast."

Russell gave a small smile. "Pacelli women are tough. It must run in the family."

Ellie grinned, glad that he seemed to be over whatever funk her escapade with the killer in Karen's office had put him in. Though of course, he had a brand-new set of worries to contend with now. It had been stupid of her to tell Alex and his brother Chris that she had witnessed Celestine's death. What had she been thinking? *Well, I wasn't thinking, that's the problem,* she mused. *I just opened my mouth and blurted everything out.*

"… tomorrow night?"

"What?" she realized that Russell had been talking while she was thinking about her encounter with the brothers, and she had missed whatever he said. "Sorry, I got lost in my thoughts."

"I was asking if you were free to have dinner tomorrow night," he said, looking amused. "I meant to call you earlier, but then Celestine's friends showed up."

"I'd love that," she said, smiling, glad that they were back to normal.

"Great, I'll pick you up at eight."

CHAPTER TEN

Ellie turned down her radio and looked in the mirror. It had taken her over an hour to get ready due to distractions from her grandmother, Bunny, and even Marlowe. The clock warned her that it was only a few minutes until eight, but since Russell hadn't called or texted her yet to let her know he was on his way, she figured she still had some time.

I wish my hair would do more than just lay there, she thought. She had always been envious of women who had voluminous, wavy hair. Still, she thought she looked okay, especially for a woman in her forties that spent more time around food than she did outside.

"What do you think, Bunny?" she asked the papillon, who was laying on the bed, watching her morosely with her head between her paws. The dog seemed to know that her owner was about to leave for the evening. "Don't give me that look. You like Russell too, you know. And Nonna's going to be here with you the whole time. It's not like I'm leaving you completely alone."

She broke off her one-sided conversation with her dog when her phone rang. *That must be Russell, calling to tell me he's on his way.* She checked the caller id, then answered it.

"Hey," she said by way of greeting.

"Ellie." She could tell by his voice that something was wrong. "I'm not going to be able to make it tonight."

"Is everything all right? What's going on?"

"Someone slashed all four tires on my truck and broke a couple of windows."

Ellie's eyes went wide. "But... you're the sheriff."

"I know." His voice was grim. "It looks like I'm going to be spending the evening going over the surveillance from the parking lot instead of taking you to dinner. I'm sorry, Ellie. Maybe we can go out Sunday evening instead."

"It's okay — I'm just glad *you're* all right. Who would do something like that? They had to know it was your car."

"I'm sure they did. You be careful, all right? This person hasn't hurt anyone yet that we know of, but that doesn't mean it won't escalate."

"It can't be random, can it?" she asked. "I mean, first Shannon, then Jacob, and now you… it seems sort of odd that three people that I know have had something like this happen. It's not like I know all that many people, Russell."

"That's another reason I want you to be careful. If this person is targeting us for a reason, and isn't doing this randomly, then you could be on his or her list as well."

With that solemn warning, he got off the line and Ellie was left with a feeling of unease in the pit of her stomach. She wasn't exactly in the mood to sit around the house, but she didn't know where else she could go. It didn't seem like a good idea to go anywhere alone just then. *Maybe Shannon's free*, she thought. *I've got a lot to talk to her about, anyway.*

It may not have been a date with Russell, but eating dinner with her best friend at the Lobster Pot was easily the next best thing. The restaurant was comfortable and crowded, and the food was mouthwatering, if not exactly healthy.

"I've told you before, Ellie, and I'm going to tell you again — you really should offer a lobster pizza at Papa Pacelli's." Shannon lifted a slice off of her plate and bit into it, closing her eyes blissfully as she chewed.

"To think I expected loyalty from you," Ellie said with a mock sigh. "You're a traitor, you know that?"

"I'll stop coming here for the pizza once you start serving something similar," her friend said. "I've got to get my lobster pizza somewhere."

The pizza did look and smell pretty good, though Ellie was refusing to try it as a matter of principle. Besides, she had her own dish to contend with — a whole lobster tail on top of a pile of Alfredo noodles, shrimp, and scallops. It was a bigger serving than she had bargained for, and probably had enough calories to sustain her for a week, judging by how rich and buttery it tasted. She didn't regret ordering it, though. As far as she was concerned, she deserved every bite of the meal. Comfort food was important when one was possibly the target of either a killer, a car vandal, or both.

"Thanks for meeting me," she said to her friend as she twirled one thick noodle around her fork. "I can't believe *another* date with Russell was wrecked."

"Good to know I'm just a backup plan," Shannon joked. "Seriously, though, I hope he catches whoever's responsible for messing up people's cars. Someone could get hurt, eventually."

"I'm sure he'll do what he can, but I'm guessing solving the murder is probably still a priority," Ellie said.

"True. And it should be." Her friend looked sobered. "Do you know if he's been making any progress with the case?"

"Actually, that's one of the reasons that I wanted to meet you. Celestine's boyfriend came into the store yesterday…"

She told her friend about the conversation she had had with the two men the day before, and her discussion with Russell that same evening. Shannon listened closely. When Ellie was done, the other woman said, "That reminds me. I've got something to tell you too."

"About the case?" Ellie asked, surprised.

Her friend nodded. "The other day, after we found out who the woman that got killed was, James told me that he had a meeting with her earlier that week. She was looking at a piece of land just outside of town, and wanted to know what it would take to have a house built on it."

James was a contractor, and owned his own company. Ellie was surprised by this news; from everything she's heard, Celestine and Alex hadn't exactly been a happy couple. "Just her?"

"Yeah, but she scheduled a second meeting and told him she was going to bring her boyfriend along." Shannon fell silent. "She, ah, never made it to that one, though."

"That's… interesting," Ellie said. She frowned. Something had just occurred to her. Jacob's tires had been slashed the day after her delivered a pizza to Celestine. Russell's tires had been slashed the day after he had spoken to Celestine's friends. "What day did he have the meeting with her?"

"Oh, it was the day before I came over to help you decorate your grandmother's house, I think."

"So the day before you got the flat?"

"Yes, it must have been."

Ellie poked her fork at her lobster tail, still hungry but too distracted to take a bite. *It can't be coincidence, can it?* she thought. *All three of them had something to do with Celestine right before their tires got slashed. I just wish I knew* why. *It must be important.*

CHAPTER ELEVEN

An icy breeze blew in from the coast, making Ellie shiver and tuck her scarf more tightly into her coat. The warm spell had ended, and the weekend had been ushered in with stormy skies and a steep drop in temperature. It really felt like November now. Even Bunny, who usually loved going outside, looked like she was beginning to feel uncomfortable.

"I'll try to find your sweater before our next walk," Ellie promised the pup. "Though you *are* wearing a fur coat. I think you're just a tiny bit spoiled."

The dog looked up at her and cocked her head to the side, her large ears like satellite dishes. The pizzeria manager smiled. She'd always adored Bunny's big ears.

"I guess we've gone far enough for today. What do you say we turn back?" She'd hoped to walk off some of the calories from her pity dinner with Shannon the evening before, but it was just too chilly for the long, leisurely walk that she had been planning on. At least all of the shivering that she's been doing should have burned up some extra energy.

Bracing herself for the wind to assault her from the opposite side, she turned around and began the walk back to the Pacelli house. It was Saturday, so she didn't have to make an appearance at the pizzeria, though she'd probably stop in anyway simply due to the fact that she couldn't think of anything more pressing to do with her evening. First, though, she had promised her grandmother that they would have a nice, home-cooked lunch together.

"I'm so glad you can spend some time around the house today," Nonna said. "I'm feeling more like my old self now. I've got my appetite back and everything."

"Well, that's good," Ellie said. "I got everything on the list you gave me. Should we get started?"

"Bring the crackers and dip out first. I didn't eat much at breakfast, and I'm starved."

Ellie looked through the shopping bags until she found the box of wheat crackers and the container of freshly made spinach and artichoke dip. She scooped the dip into a bowl, arranged half of the crackers on a plate, and set the food in the middle of the kitchen table. She wasn't sure exactly what had her grandmother in such a good mood, but she was glad for it.

"I'll start on the soup," she told the older woman. "Save me some dip."

She pulled the printed-out recipe for creamy chicken and dumpling soup out of her purse and set it on the counter next to the stove. She could already tell that it was going to be filling and warming — perfect for such a chilly, overcast day.

By the time the soup was ready to serve, the kitchen smelled heavenly and Ellie's stomach was grumbling. She grabbed a cracker from the platter on the table, scooped up some dip, and popped it into her mouth before reaching up into the cabinets for the nice set of dishes that Nonna had requested they use. She was beginning to suspect that her grandmother was up to something, and hadn't the faintest idea what.

At last she had put the finishing touches to the place settings, ladled a serving of soup into each of their bowls, and had tossed the salad with the balsamic vinaigrette dressing after spending ages digging through the pantry for it. She sat down, already feeling tired even though it was still early afternoon.

"There you go." She gave her grandmother a small smiled. "Everything you asked for."

"It looks just wonderful, dear. Thank you so much. I would have done it myself, of course, but with my arm... well, it's not very easy to cook with only one hand free. But I wanted something special for this."

Nonna reached for her purse, which was on the chair beside her, and pulled out a manila file folder. Ellie watched her with rising curiosity and some trepidation. What was her grandmother up to?

"You take a look at this and tell me what you think," she said, handing the folder over.

Ellie took it, and, as her grandmother began eating, opened it. It took her a few moments to realize what she was looking at.

"Nonna... what is this? I don't understand..."

"All it needs is your signature, dear."

"I can't accept this… the pizzeria is yours. Papa opened it, and it's right that you have it now."

"Oh, Ellie." The older woman sighed and put down her spoon. "I'm getting old. No, I *am* old, and I've really been feeling it lately. I'm not going to be around forever. I could leave it to you in my will, but I'd rather give it to you now, while I'm around to see you flourish as a business owner. I'm giving you the pizzeria, Ellie. All you have to do is sign."

Ellie stared at the documents in front of her, speechless. Papa Pacelli's… hers. She wouldn't just be the manager anymore, but the owner. It wouldn't change much, really, but at the same time it would change everything. Was she prepared to own a business? Half the time she felt like she didn't have a clue what she was doing while she was running the place.

"What about taxes and insurance?" she asked.

"The accountant your grandfather hired takes care of all of that," her grandmother said. "Really, Ellie, it's all taken care of. It was dreadful, trying to find the time to schedule a meeting with the lawyer to get these papers drawn up. I wanted to surprise you, see, so I had to go while you were at work. Gertie gave me a ride, dear thing. She's a wonderful friend, you know."

"I know," Ellie said distractedly. She was still staring at the file, her hunger forgotten. It didn't seem like it would be right to sign it. How could she know that Nonna was in her right mind? Maybe the pain medication or her antibiotics were effecting her mind. *This took a lot of planning*, a little voice in the back of Ellie's mind said. *It's not something she could do impulsively.* "I just wouldn't feel right taking it, Nonna."

"You'd better sign it, Eleanora Pacelli, or you'll be letting me down. I want this business to stay in the family, and the only way I can make sure it gets into the right hands is by figuring out all of this legal mumbo-jumbo while I still have half a brain to do it."

Nonna's gaze was steady and serious. Taking a deep breath, Ellie nodded and reached for the pen that was clipped to the papers. Her hand shaking slightly, she signed and initialed each line that the lawyer had highlighted. The pizzeria was hers.

CHAPTER TWELVE

"Oh my goodness, Ellie, that's wonderful!" Shannon squealed and seized her in a tight hug. "I can't believe it. This place is yours now? You could do anything you want to it?"

"Yeah." Ellie grinned at her friend. "Well, technically it's not mine until I turn the papers in to the lawyer on Monday."

She still felt a little bit guilty about signing, as if she had somehow taken advantage of her grandmother by doing so. Still, it wasn't as if she was going to do anything drastic now that she owned the place. She had nothing but good intentions.

Ellie looked around herself fondly. They were standing in the middle of the pizzeria's dining area, which was thankfully empty at the moment. Shannon was walking around the room, touching everything as if she had never seen it before. Rose and Iris were in the kitchen; she hadn't told them about the change in ownership yet, and wasn't quite sure how to bring it up so that she didn't sound as if she was bragging. She had signed the papers only hours before, and it still felt somewhat unreal.

"I'm glad you stopped by," she said to her friend. "I was just about to call you when you showed up, in fact."

"Oh! That reminds me. I didn't just happen to drop by. I was hoping you'd be in." Shannon glanced towards the kitchen and lowered her voice. "You'll never guess who tracked me down earlier today while I was hanging around the editor's office at the paper."

"Who?"

"One of the two brothers that you told me about. Christopher Gaines."

"Really?" Ellie's eyes widened. "What in the world did he want?"

"He heard that I was with you when you saw the murderer and wanted to ask me some questions. He asked to meet somewhere more private than the office. And get this." She lowered her voice even further. "He said he didn't want his brother getting wind of any of this."

"That's really odd, Shannon. Did you tell Russell?"

"I want to hear what he has to say first. I mean, if he wanted to see the sheriff, he'd just go do it himself, wouldn't he? It's not like the sheriff's department is hard to find."

"What if he's dangerous, Shannon?" Ellie shook her head. "Where did you tell him you'd meet him?"

"Ah… here. In about five minutes."

Fighting down a surge of annoyance at her friend — she understood her curiosity, but in her opinion this entire situation could have been handled much better — Ellie went into the kitchen and let her employees know that she was going to be having lunch with Shannon and someone else, so she wouldn't be minding the register.

She hoped that Chris wouldn't show up. She wasn't quite sure why she thought meeting with him was such a bad idea. Maybe it was just because Russell had so recently impressed upon her how important it was for her to be careful. *I'll just have to hope that Shannon knows what she's doing*, she thought. *There he is now.*

"You're sure this is off the record? I don't want any of it in the paper." Chris glanced pointedly at Shannon

"My lips are sealed," she promised.

He still looked doubtful, but took a deep breath and began speaking anyway. "I think my brother is the one who killed Celestine."

"Really?" Ellie said, surprised. Sure, those women who had been friends of Celestine sure seemed to think that he had done something, but she still couldn't shake the feeling that Alex's grief had been sincere when she'd last seen him.

Chris nodded. "I wouldn't say anything if I didn't have good reason for my suspicions. The man's my family, after all. That's why I don't want to go to the sheriff until I'm absolutely sure."

"Why'd you want to talk to us?" Shannon asked. "We don't know anything other than what the cops know. We probably know a lot less, in fact."

"But you witnessed it," Chris said, keeping his voice low and urgent. "You two are the only ones besides Celestine that saw the killer and, well, she's not talking. Surely you must remember *something* about the man who killed her?"

"It happened so quickly," Ellie said, shaking her head slowly. "I really don't remember anything about him other than what he was wearing, and I didn't even see his clothes for more than an instant as he ran past the window. I wouldn't even be able to pick him out of a line-up."

"Me either," her friend added. "I think I was even more frozen than Ellie. At least she tried to help Celestine after the attacker fled. I could barely even manage to dial nine-one-one."

"So you didn't see *anything?*" he pressed. Both of them shook their heads. He sighed and made to stand up. "Thanks for meeting me anyway, I guess."

"Hold on," Ellie said. "We may not be able to help you identify her killer, but there is something else I noticed that seems odd to me."

Chris sat back down. "Go on."

Shannon looked at her questioningly. "Yeah, go on, Ellie. This is the first time I've heard of anything else."

"Well, you know how your tire got slashed that day you came over to decorate?" Her friend nodded. "That was the day after James met with Celestine to talk about the house she was thinking of building. And Jacob's car got messed up the day after he delivered the pizza to her. And someone did the same thing to Russell's truck the day after he spoke to Celestine's friends. All three of those people had ties to her just before someone sabotaged their vehicles. Can that really be a coincidence?"

Chris frowned, his forehead creased with concentration as he took in what she said. Shannon, on the other hand, shook her head.

"Ellie, other people have had their tires slashed too. That older guy at the bistro, remember? He probably didn't know Celestine at all. It's just some vandal who enjoys playing pranks on people."

"What old guy?" Chris interrupted. "What did he look like?"

"Balding, a bit round. He drove a red sports car," Shannon told him.

"That sounds like Mr. Fischer. He was Celestine's boss."

The three of them fell silent as they took that in. Ellie was convinced that her hunch was right. The vandalism was connected to the murder. But why?

"Why do you think it was your brother?" she asked Chris after a moment. "You said you had a good reason for your suspicions. What is it?"

"Because Celestine was cheating on him," Chris said. "She thought he didn't know, but he did. He was obsessed with her — still is, in fact. I think he finally snapped and decided to end her instead of ending their relationship."

CHAPTER THIRTEEN

Ellie was shaken from her conversation with Chris and Shannon, but went home that evening without telling Russell. She wanted to figure out who that Mr. Fischer was first, and see if he was the same person that had seen his car get vandalized at the bistro. She'd had enough experience with being the woman who called wolf, and didn't want to waste the sheriff's time again if she could help it.

When she began her search for Mr. Fischer online, she expected it to take only a few minutes, but it turned out that Fischer was a rather common last name in the area. Without a first name, or any clue what sort of business he had run, finding him online would be a daunting if not impossible task. *I bet Russell knows where Celestine worked*, she thought. *I'll ask him at dinner tonight, then we'll probably be able to track down a picture of the man.* If Celestine's boss *hadn't* been the man in the bistro, then she knew that her theory about the car vandal and the murders being connected wouldn't stand up to scrutiny. Still embarrassed about how wrong she'd been in the past, she decided to bring the topic up as naturally as possible that evening. She was determined not to let *anything* wreck this date.

She got ready that evening with a sense of Deja vu. Bunny was lying on her bed in almost exactly the same spot, watching her sadly as she examined herself in the mirror. When her phone rang at a quarter to eight, she half expected Russell to cancel again. She was relieved when he told her instead that he was on his way.

Russell had made reservations not for the White Pine Kitchen, but rather at a nice restaurant in Benton Harbor called Juliette's. The drive was a good forty minutes, and by the time they got there, thoughts of the murder and the car vandal had been pushed to the side by hunger. The restaurant was beautiful, with a comfortable, Italian feel.

They perused their menus and placed their orders. It wasn't until the appetizer came — freshly made flatbread with a smoked whitefish dip — that Ellie could focus on the news that she most wanted to share with the sheriff. Opening her purse, she withdrew a manila folder and handed it over to him. Raising his eyebrows, he opened it and looked inside. She saw the exact moment that he realized what he was seeing, and met his grin with one of her own.

"Your grandmother's giving you the pizzeria?"

She nodded. "I can hardly believe it myself. When I first came here, I just planned on helping out for a while. I never thought I'd end up owning the place. I still feel very conflicted about agreeing to sign. I don't want to take advantage of my grandmother. What if she wasn't thinking straight when she came up with all of this?"

"I don't think you have to worry about that. She's probably been planning this for a while."

"You think so?"

"I do. It makes sense for her to want to keep the restaurant in the family and, well, she doesn't have any other family around here, does she? And over the past few months, you've proven that you can do amazing things. The restaurant is nearly unrecognizable now compared to how it was a year ago, and in a good way." He smiled at her. "So, congratulations, Ellie. Papa Pacelli's is yours. You shouldn't waste any time feeling bad about that."

She smiled, glad that she had told Russell before she'd had time to agonize with her feelings of guilt any longer. He was right; it made sense for Nonna to want to find a good owner for the pizzeria before she lost her ability to do so. "Thanks," she told him. "That means a lot to me."

"So, what did your employees say when you told them?" he asked.

"I actually haven't said anything to them yet," she admitted. "Shannon's the only other person who knows. I told her yesterday evening when she stopped by the pizzeria."

That reminded her of the other topic she wanted to bring up; that of Chris and his brother, Alex. She bit her lip. Their date was going so well. Would bringing up Celestine's murder wreck it? She would just have to do this carefully, that was all.

"Have you had any luck tracking down the person who trashed your car?" she asked. It wasn't exactly a smooth change of subject, but hopefully he wouldn't notice.

"No." He sighed. "The security footage caught the person on tape, of course, but there's no way to identify the culprit. He — or she — was wearing a ski mask, and didn't touch anything, so there's no hope of getting fingerprints."

"A ski mask?" Ellie asked, her heart starting to pound. "Like the guy who killed Celestine?"

Russell stared at her, his brows drawing together. "Yes, but a lot of criminals wear something to hide their identity. The chance of it being the same person..." He trailed off. She could see him connecting the dots in his mind.

"You, Jacob, and Shannon — through James — all had some sort of connection with Celestine," she said. "That can't be a coincidence."

"It *could* be a coincidence," he said. "Never say never. But you're on to something. I just don't understand what the motivation would be."

"Me either," she said.

Russell put down the glass of water that he had just picked up, without taking a sip first. His gaze locked onto hers. "You sound like you've been giving this a lot of thought," he said.

"It's crossed my mind a few times," she said.

"Ellie, didn't I tell you to be careful? You're supposed to leave the whole investigating crimes thing to me. Getting involved could be dangerous for you, especially since you witnessed the crime in question."

"Just *thinking* about something isn't going to hurt me," she said. She decided not to mention her and Shannon's meeting with Chris unless she had to. "And it's sort of hard not to think about it when two of my friends and one of my employees all got their tires slashed within day of each other."

He shook his head, as if to clear it. "You're right," he said. "I'm sorry. I know I worry too much. I do think you're onto something, but I'll have to look into it more. Let's just enjoy our dinner for now."

"Okay," she agreed. *I still haven't told him about Mr. Fischer,* she thought. *Chris seemed pretty certain that he was the guy at the bistro. It might be an important connection.* She was reluctant to bring up the subject of Celestine again, though. The sheriff must have spent nearly every moment for the past week thinking about her, pouring over the case, trying to solve her murder; it didn't seem fair to make him talk about it on their date as well.

"Are you planning on making any changes to the pizzeria, now that it's going to be yours?" he asked, getting back to their original topic.

"No, not that I can think of. Honestly, it won't be much of a change. I'm happy with how well it's doing now. I think I'm going to continue expanding the menu, but we've already been doing that."

"What else are you going to add?" he asked.

In the past few weeks alone, she had already added both calzones and brownies to the menu, and both had been successful. She felt like she was on a roll. "Salads, for one. Nothing fancy, but I think people would order them if we had them. And I think I'm going to look into getting a gluten free recipe for our dough, as well. It was popular option for pizza places back in Chicago, and it can't hurt to give it a try here."

"Both of those sound like great ideas. I'd —" He broke off as his phone rang. He stared at it for a moment, then sighed and picked it up off the table. "I'm sorry, Ellie, but it's a call from the department."

"It's fine," she told him. "I understand."

She ate more of the smoked whitefish appetizer while he spoke to whoever was on the other line, thinking of her plans for the pizzeria. She wanted to stay loyal to Arthur Pacelli's original concept, but still keep the restaurant as up to date and modern as possible. Maybe they should implement an online ordering system... then again, that might just complicate matters. There was a difference between updating things that needed it, and trying to fix something that wasn't broken.

"We've got to go," Russell said, startling her out of her thoughts. "That was Mrs. Laffere. The car vandal has struck again, but this time someone caught him in the act. I have his license plate number and the make and model of his vehicle. With any luck, I'll be able to track him down and maybe even get some answers about Celestine's death while I'm at it."

CHAPTER FOURTEEN

With time being of the essence, Russell was forced to let Ellie ride along with him. She was thrilled, though he seemed less than happy with the arrangement. With the lights on top of the truck flashing, they flew through the night, following the state highway along the coast back up to Kittiport.

"Whatever happens, I want you to stay in the car," he said. "Do you understand?"

She nodded. "Where are we going?"

He glanced over at her. "The call came from the house that Celestine was staying at," he said. "It's another connection to her, a strong one. I think you were right, Ellie. It's no coincidence that the person slashing tires and breaking windows is targeting people that are connected to her."

Ellie couldn't help the triumphant feeling that blossomed in her chest. She had been right, for once. She'd managed to piece together something of a mystery without being dreadfully wrong, and it was a good feeling.

"Who lived at the house with her?" she asked.

"The house is owned by the Gaines brothers," he said. "She didn't live there permanently, but split her time between there and Portland, which is why she hadn't changed her address."

"What was in Portland?"

"Her job," he said, keeping his eyes on the road as he navigated a curve in the road. "She worked as an actress for an advertising firm. She got called down for a week or two every month to do a shoot for the next advertisement."

Ellie fell silent, digesting this information. If Celestine's job had been in Portland, then what had her boss been doing in Kittiport? Of course, she still hadn't confirmed that the man in the bistro had indeed been Mr. Fischer, but if all of the other car vandal incidents had been connected, it stood to reason that that one had been, too. So, what reason did Mr. Fischer have to spend a day in Kittiport?

"We're close," Russell said. "Keep your eyes open. We're looking for an older car, dark blue." He recited the license plate number. "Two people looking is better than one, since I've got to concentrate on the road as well. Mrs. Laffere said the person who called in reported that the car drove away to the north. Bethany and Liam are covering the roads in town. We'll take the back roads."

They passed Celestine's old house in a rush, and Russell turned off the flashing lights. Ellie kept her eyes peeled, but there was no sign of any other cars on the road at all. She realized that if the car had come from the house where Celestine had lived with the two brothers, then one of them must have made the call. What was going on? She wished Russell had given her more information, but she didn't want to distract him by asking now. This was turning out to be quite the exciting date.

"Wait, I think I saw something back there," Ellie said suddenly. "Headlights, down that dirt road we passed."

Russell turned the truck around in the road and went back. They rounded a bend in the road just in time to see a car turning off of the dirt road and onto the main highway. The vehicle was heading back the way they had come, towards the Gaines brothers' house. The sheriff increased his speed, coming up behind the car close enough so they could read the license plate.

"That's him," he said. He turned the flashing lights back on. Ellie, who was half prepared for a chase scene like in the movies, was surprised when the vehicle slowed down and pulled over without hesitation.

"Stay here," Russell said firmly as he unbuckled his seatbelt and got out of the truck. He withdrew a large, heavy flashlight from under his seat and flicked it on.

She watched in mute fascination as he approached the car and shone the light in, looking first through the front window, then into the back seat. He took something from the driver — Ellie assumed it was the person's insurance and registration — and looked it over before handing it back. He gestured, and the driver's door opened. Someone stepped out. She leaned forward, trying to see who it was, but it was dark and Russell was still aiming his flashlight at the car.

The driver put his hand on the car and stood while the sheriff patted him down for weapons. Then Russell reached inside the vehicle and a second later the trunk popped open. He walked slowly around to the back, opened the truck the rest of the way, and shone the flashlight inside.

At that moment, the car's driver ran into the woods.

Ellie could hear Russell swear through the glass. She saw him unclip his radio from his belt and bring it to his mouth. *Probably calling for backup,* she thought. He turned and held up his hand in a gesture that very clearly was telling her to wait, then turned and ran into the trees in pursuit of the driver.

She made a good effort to wait in the truck, but after a few minutes' curiosity overwhelmed her sense of responsibility. The trunk was wide open. How could she *not* look? Besides, it wasn't like she would be in any danger. There was no one else around, and Bethany and Liam were bound to get there soon.

"Just one peek," she said to herself as she unbuckled her seatbelt. "Then I'll get back in the truck and wait, just like Russell wanted."

She left the truck's door open as she walked down the gravel shoulder of the road, pausing to turn her cell phone's flashlight app on before she shone the light into the car's trunk. She was both disappointed and relieved by what she saw. There wasn't anything gruesome, just a bundle of black clothing.

Ellie was about to turn off the flashlight app and return to the heated interior of the truck when she realized the importance of what she was looking at. Black clothing. Could it be the same clothing that Celestine's killer or the car vandal had worn? Her curiosity renewed, she prodded the bundle of clothes until she managed to separate the pieces. Sure enough, there was a ski mask, and not only that, but there was something hard in the pocket of the sweatshirt that turned out to be a folding pocket knife.

Even though she knew that she should go back to Russell's truck and wait there, it was impossible to curb her curiosity. Ellie walked up to the driver's door and peered in the open window. She saw a pile of papers, and leaned closer. It was the registration and insurance that the driver had handed to Russell. She recognized the name on them immediately. The car belonged to Alexander Gaines.

CHAPTER FIFTEEN

*A*lex must have been behind it all, she thought. Everything seemed to fall into place. *What Chris said was true — he must have been totally obsessed with Celestine. He killed her attacked all of the men that she had contact with.* She shivered, suddenly feeling the cold November air more keenly. She was worried about Russell now. Someone as unstable as Alex might be a real danger to him.

She heard the sound of an engine and turned moments before a car rounded the bend from the direction of town. She felt a rush of relief. It was probably one of the deputies, here to give Russell the backup that he needed. The car slowed and parked behind the sheriff's truck. Ellie put her phone in her pocket and walked towards it, only to stumble to a halt a few feet away when she was able to see the vehicle more clearly past the headlights. It was the wrong color to be one of the deputies' cars.

Feeling a swirl of fear in her stomach, she took a step backwards as the driver's side door opened. A tall, dark shape unfolded itself from inside, but she didn't recognize him until he stepped in front of the headlights.

"Chris," she gasped, relieved that it was someone she knew. "What are you doing here?"

"I saw my brother's car." He nodded towards the dark blue vehicle with its trunk wide open. "Is he okay? Did he get into an accident?"

"No, he was pulled over." She took a deep breath "I think you were right. About him killing Celestine."

He closed his eyes and turned his face away from her for a moment. She wondered what he was thinking. She had never had a sibling, but she could imagine that it must be hard to learn something so terrible about a family member that he was so close to.

"I'm sorry," she said softly.

"It's all right." He sighed and sat down on the hood of his car. "I was expecting it, but still, to hear it out loud…" he shook his head. "Where is he?"

"He ran into the woods," Ellie said. "Russ — the sheriff — is looking for him. Backup will be here soon."

"Into the woods?" Chris asked. "Did you see which direction he was headed?"

"Um, that way, I think," she said, pointing.

"He's heading back towards the house," he muttered. "Crap."

"I'm sure they'll catch him, even if he makes it to the house."

"That's what I'm worried about." He sighed and stood up. "I'm going to head there and see if I can intercept him. You coming?"

"I don't know, I was supposed to stay here…" she said hesitantly.

"I don't think it's safe for you to stay here on your own. What if he circles back?"

"Well… okay." He had a point. Alex was obviously not in his right mind, and she wouldn't feel safe waiting alone in the truck for Russell to return or the deputies to show up. At least with Chris, there would be safety in numbers.

She got into the passenger seat of his car and looked out the window, feeling bad for leaving without saying anything to Russell. If he came back and saw that she was gone, he would be worried. Still, the thought of being alone on the side of the road if Alex came back was simply terrifying. She would have no way to defend herself. There might be a gun somewhere in the sheriff's truck, but she would have no idea how to use it safely.

"You ready?" Chris asked. She nodded. He put the car into gear and pulled out from behind the sheriff's truck. Soon they were speeding down the road towards the Gaines brothers' house.

Before long, Chris put on his turn signal and pulled up the gravel drive to the large, but slightly run down looking house. The windows were dark, and there was no sign of anyone in the yard.

"You wait here," Chris said. "I'm going to go make sure he's not in the house. If you see anyone come out of the trees, yell."

Ellie nodded mutely, feeling slightly annoyed that once again she was being asked to wait in the car like someone's pet. Still, she couldn't deny that she was glad that she didn't have to walk through a stranger's home looking for a murderer.

After Chris left, she kept her eyes glued to the tree line. Where was Russell? Was he still chasing Alex? Had he caught him yet? Were they on their way back to the road, or was the sheriff lying in a pool of his own blood in that dark forest somewhere?

As more and more time passed, the anxiety and concern kept growing inside of her. *Something* should have happened by now. It couldn't take that long for Alex to run from his car through the woods to the house. It would be a straight shot through the forest, much shorter than taking the road, which curved in a big loop around this section of trees. If Russell had managed to catch the other man, then surely they would be back at the truck by now. Once the sheriff noticed that she was missing, he was bound to call her.

Ellie checked her cellphone for what felt like the hundredth time, but there was still no sign that Russell had tried to contact her. She had considered texting him herself, just to let him know where she was, but she didn't remember seeing him turn his phone volume down, and didn't want to jeopardize his safety by sending him a message at the wrong time.

And what was taking Chris so long, anyway? He had turned a couple of lights on in the house, and now she could see him walking past a window on the upper floor. It didn't seem like he could still be searching for Alex, and she was tired of sitting in the car and doing nothing.

Making up her mind, Ellie undid her seatbelt, shoved her phone into her pocket, and got out of the car. At least inside she wouldn't be a sitting duck if Alex did show up, and maybe she could even convince Chris to tell her more about his brother. She still couldn't figure out what, exactly, had driven him over the edge and caused him to end things with his girlfriend once and for all.

CHAPTER SIXTEEN

Ellie opened the front door cautiously and stepped through. The first thing she noticed was that the house was a mess. A picture frame hung crookedly off the wall, its glass shattered. A small table in the entranceway had been knocked over, and the drywall at the foot of the stairs had been caved in. It almost looked like someone had kicked it.

"Chris?" she called out. She heard something fall upstairs. Feeling uncomfortable and beginning to wish that she had stayed in the car after all, she tentatively walked up the first couple of steps. *What happened here?* she wondered. *It looks like someone went on a rampage.* Maybe Alex was even crazier than she had thought, though why he would take his anger out on his own house, she had no idea.

Beginning to feel concerned for Chris, she continued up the stairs. At least the upper story didn't look like a hurricane had raged through it. Only one room had a light on, so she headed that direction. She knocked on the doorframe a second before poking her head around it.

"Chris, it was taking so long I started to get worried —" She broke off mid-sentence. "What are you doing?"

He was throwing clothes into a suitcase, and it looked like he already had a second one packed and ready to go. He looked up when she came in and his expression hardened, but other than that he didn't acknowledge her presence.

"What are you doing?" she repeated. "Are you packing?"

"Yes," he said shortly. "You should have waited in the car like I asked."

"Well I wanted to make sure you were okay. And I hate just sitting there without being able to help. What in the world happened downstairs?"

"Alex." Chris's face was a sneer.

"Did he get here before us?"

"He did that earlier today."

"Oh." Ellie fell silent, watching him continue to inexplicable shove all of his possessions into the suitcase. Something occurred to her. "Wait, Russell told me that the original call to the police came from this house. Was that you?"

He put down the shirt that he had been attempting to fold and looked up at her. His expression was cold, and there was something in his eyes that Ellie didn't like.

"I've got to say, I'm a bit surprised that it took you that long to figure it out," he said. "Yes, I called the police on my brother. He came in here with his fists swinging, looking for a fight. I pulled a knife and he took off. I thought the police would at least be competent enough to catch one guy, but I guess I was wrong."

"But *why* did Alex attack you?" she asked. "Did he find out that you think he killed Celestine."

A grim grin broke out across Chris's face. "No. He found out that I'm the one that had been sleeping with his girlfriend."

A stunned silence fell. After a moment, Ellie said, "Well, that was terrible of you." Chris just shrugged and continued packing.

Ellie turned and was about to head back downstairs when she heard the front door slam open. Chris swore loudly behind her, and a moment later she felt his fingers close around her arm. He yanked her back into the bedroom and shut the door.

"Get in the corner," he said. "Don't try to leave, or you'll be sorry."

Her heart pounding, Ellie did as she was told. Chris went back to the bed and began frantically trying to zip up his overstuffed suitcase. She heard the sound of footsteps coming up the stairs.

"Chris —" she began, but he cut her off.

"Shut up. Just do what I say. Come over to the window and crawl out onto the roof."

"No, don't be stupid —"

"What did I say?" he growled, rounding on her. She heard the metallic sound of a pocket knife opening and glanced down to see a blade in his hand. She gulped.

At that moment, the doorknob twisted and rattled as someone tried to open it. Ellie knew that the little lock on the handle wouldn't hold if the person on the other side was determined about getting in. Her eyes flitted from the door to Chris's menacing frame in front of her.

She was trapped between two dangerous people, but only one of them was a murderer.

"Okay," she whispered to Chris. "Okay, I'll do it. Just put the knife down."

She walked over to the window and pulled it open. It took her a moment to figure out how to get the screen out. She had just popped it out of the frame when she saw two, no, three sets of headlights pull into the driveway.

"Not enough time," Chris muttered darkly from just over her shoulder. "Get between me and the door. Now."

Confused and terrified, she did as she was told just as the bedroom door burst open. Alex stood behind it, leaves and twigs in his hair and his hands shaking.

"Leave her be, Chris," he said. "Face me like a man. Ellie, hurry up and get away from him."

"No way," Ellie said, her voice coming out more squeaky and high pitched than she expected. "You killed Celestine. Why would I think you wouldn't do the same to me?"

"I didn't kill her!" Alex shouted, his eyes wild. "My brother did, and he's going to do the same to you if you don't get away from him."

"That's not true. I know you killed her, I figured it all out. She was cheating on you, and you didn't know with who at first so you tried to scare off every guy that she had contact with, but you just couldn't stand it, could you, so you stabbed her!"

"Only half of that is right," Alex said. He was easing slowly into the room. "I admit to trying to scare off the guys that she saw, and it was stupid of me. At first I was just mad, but after she died I thought the best way to solve her murder would be to find her killer. She went to break up with him earlier that day, you see. She wanted to start over with me. She never told me who it was, but she swore to me that it was over. So yeah, I made a list of all of the guys she'd seen over the past couple of weeks and stalked them for a while. Pretty soon I realized that none of them were the right guy. But I'd never hurt Celestine. You've got to believe me."

"Why would you slash the sheriff's tires?" Ellie asked, beginning to be convinced by his story but still full of questions. "He'd never even spoken to her."

"I didn't," Alex said, looking puzzled. His eyes flashed behind her, to his brother. "Was that you, Chris? You might as well come clean. I'm your brother, man, I deserve to know."

"It was me," Chris said through gritted teeth. "I figured out you were obsessing over finding her secret lover, and guessed you were the one messing up people's cars. I thought if I brought your little tire slashing habit to light by doing the sheriff's car, he'd track you down and see how mentally unstable you were. Then you'd be carted away and I'd be free. You took my ski mask, you jerk. Did you ever guess it was the same one I was wearing when I killed her?"

Alex paled, and Ellie gasped. "*You* killed her? But why?" she said, spinning around to stare at Chris with horror.

"She dumped me for my wimpy little brother, and to make matters even worse, she was planning on telling you." His face twisted. "She broke my heart, so I stabbed her through hers."

A sudden motion from behind her, and Ellie just had enough time to stumble backwards and out of the way as Alex ran forward and punched his brother in the face.

It was impossible for her to follow the fight that ensued. The men tumbled closer and closer to her, and Ellie continued backing up until she felt the bottom of the window frame bite into her legs. There was the flash of a knife, and someone's blood spattered her pants. With a horrified moan, she climbed backwards out the window and onto the relative safety of the roof.

"Ellie!"

She glanced down and saw Russell on the ground, looking up at her, fear evident in his pale face.

"They're fighting!" she said. "Alex didn't kill her, his brother did, but Chris has a knife and —"

She slipped on a mossy shingle and felt herself fall. Waving her arms frantically, she tried to restore her balance, but to no avail. She took a step backwards, felt nothing but air under her foot, and fell.

EPILOGUE

"Two Pacelli women in the hospital in under two weeks," Nonna said, chuckling. "Maybe they should name this room after us."

"I don't care what they name after me as long the doctor shows up soon with more medicine," Ellie groaned. "My head's killing me. I feel terrible. I can't believe they're going to make me stay here over Thanksgiving."

"I'm sure he'll be here soon, dear." The older woman patted her on the elbow. "And don't you worry about Thanksgiving. I've already cancelled the dinner with the ladies. I'm going to make the two of us a special meal and eat it here with you."

"Oh, no, Nonna, I can't let you do that – "

"Nonsense. Thanksgiving is about family. I'm not going to let you spend it here alone. Now, don't argue. The doctor will be here any minute, and he's not going to thank me for getting you riled up." As if in response to her words, a knock sounded at the door to her room.

Ellie sat up in bed while her grandmother walked over to the door. She opened it to reveal, not the doctor, but Shannon, James, and Russell.

"Oh, I'll let you three have a few minutes alone with her," Nonna said. "I'm going to go see if they have any of that wonderful gelatin left. This place has the best lime gelatin."

The moment she left, Shannon rushed over to Ellie's bed and stared down at her. "Are you okay? Do you remember your name and everything? Does it hurt terribly?"

"Yes it hurts, though it's bearable, and no, I don't have amnesia," she told her friend. "I'm fine, thanks to our sheriff."

She smiled at Russell, who gave her a pained sort of smile back. "I think what you mean to say, is that you're fine despite the sheriff irresponsibly taking you along on a call and leaving you to fend for yourself on an abandoned stretch of road with a killer on the loose."

"Don't you dare blame yourself for any of this," Ellie told him. "Seriously. If I had just stayed in the car like you'd asked, I would have been fine." She struggled to sit up further, and Shannon helped her, fluffing her pillows and propping them up behind her back. "So did you manage to catch Chris?"

"We did," Russell said. "He managed to get out to the road with one of his suitcases and was in the process of trying to hitch a ride. Luckily he was covered in blood and no one was willing to stop for him. We think his plan was to go to Canada. He must have gotten spooked when he realized that Alex might lead us back to the house, where we would have seen evidence of their earlier fight."

"How is Alex?" she asked. "Was he hurt badly?"

"He has some superficial cuts," Russell said. "But he'll be fine. He's in custody right now. He may not have killed anyone, but he still did take a knife to multiple tires and he fled during a traffic stop. Despite all of that, he seems like a good guy. He'll probably get let off with probation and community service."

"Good," Ellie said firmly. "I'm glad he's okay."

"We're glad *you're* okay," Shannon said. "You fell off a roof. You could have died."

141

"Russell caught me," Ellie pointed out.

"I partially caught you. Thankfully I managed to keep you from becoming a stain on the driveway, but you still hit your head pretty hard on the deck railing. It's amazingly lucky that you're mostly unhurt."

"Pacelli women are tough," Ellie said with a smile as she thought of her grandmother. "It takes a lot to keep us down."

Made in the USA
Lexington, KY
10 September 2018